W9-BVG-042

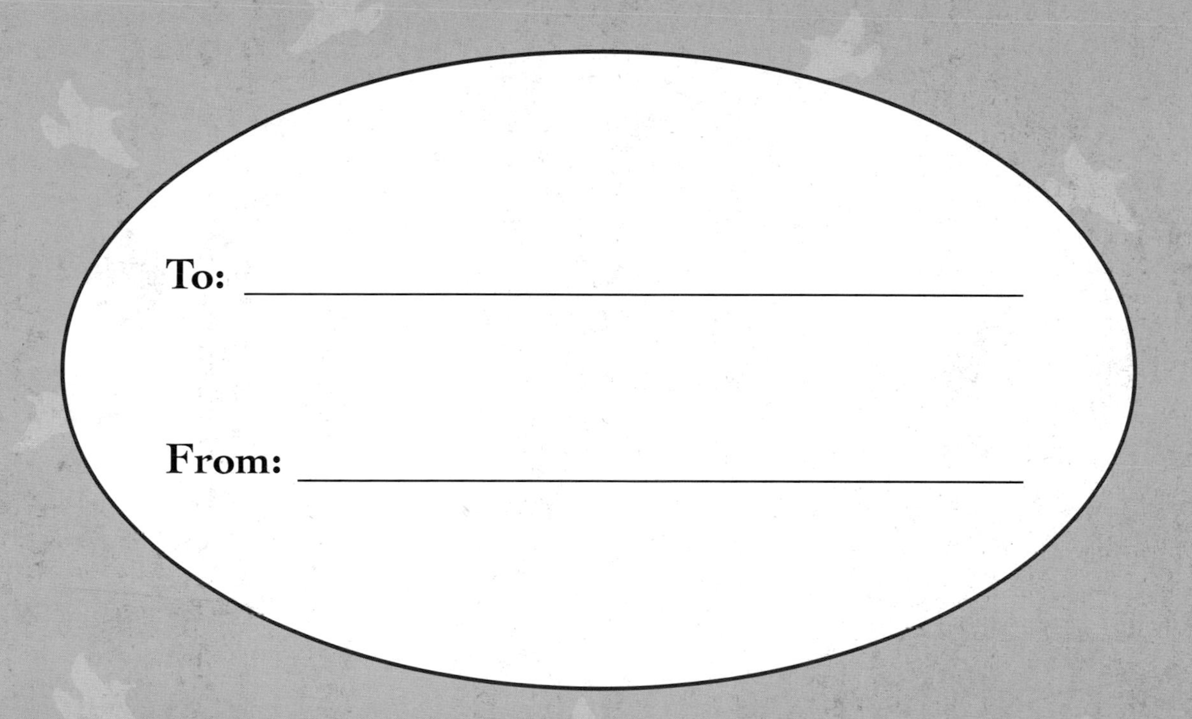
To:
From:

**"God is love."**
**—1 John 4:8**



Visit us on the Web!
rhcbooks.com
BerenstainBears.com

Educators and librarians, for a variety of teaching tools, visit us at RHTeachersLibrarians.com

Library of Congress Control Number: 2020942191
ISBN 978-0-593-30250-7 (trade) — ISBN 978-0-593-30525-6 (ebook)

MANUFACTURED IN CHINA
10 9 8 7 6 5 4 3 2 1

The Berenstain Bears®

# Gifts of the Spirit

# Love

Mike Berenstain

Based on the characters created by
Stan and Jan Berenstain



Random House New York

The Bear family, who lived down a sunny dirt road deep in Bear Country, loved each other very much! After all, Mama, Papa, Sister, Brother, and little Honey were a family. And isn't that what families do—look after each other, care for each other, and love one another?

There were other members of the Bear family, too, like Grizzly Gramps and Grizzly Gran.

"Hello there, Gramps! Hello, Gran!" the cubs called as they passed their grandparents' house.

And there were more—Cousin Fred, Uncle Ned, Aunt Min, and baby Teddi.

"Hey, Fred! Hi, Uncle Ned! Hiya, Aunt Min and Teddi!" said the cubs as they spotted their relatives on the way to school. They were all part of the family circle. They all loved each other, as well.

But not every bear in Bear Country was part of the family. How did Mama, Papa, Sister, Brother, and Honey feel about those other bears? Did they love them, too?

A day would soon come when they'd learn the answer.

Before long, it was Meet-Your-Neighbor Day in Bear Country. There was going to be a big get-together in the town square. Everyone in Bear Country was invited!

TOWN HALL
LIBRARY
MEET-YOUR-
NEIGHBOR DAY
Potluck
Supper
Come one,
come all!

Each family was asked to bring food to share. Mama, Papa, and the cubs prepared their favorite dish, honey-baked salmon, before setting off. Folks from all over Bear Country streamed into the town square.

The Bear family saw many of their friends and neighbors, including Lizzy Bruin and her family.

"Hi, Sister! Hi, Brother! Hi, Honey!" said Lizzy. "What's that? Honey-baked salmon? Yum, my favorite!"

The cubs waved to Farmer Ben and Mrs. Ben.
"Hello, young'uns!" said Farmer Ben.
"My, how you've grown!" said Mrs. Ben.

The cubs saw Preacher Brown and Mrs. Brown with their grown-up daughter and son.

"Hello there, cubs!" said Preacher Brown. "I hope you're having a blessed day!"

It was easy to feel warm and loving toward these folks they knew so well. They were just like members of their own family.

There was happy talk and laughter as the bears greeted each other and the food was set out on picnic tables.

Then Brother, Sister, and Honey began to notice many new folks they had never seen before. These bears talked and dressed differently. The food they had brought was different, too.

"Mama, Papa!" said the cubs. "Who are all these different bears? We don't recognize them."

Mama and Papa explained. “These are new neighbors who’ve just moved to Bear Country. They used to live far away. But they needed to find new homes. They traveled here from all around the world!”

Curiously, the cubs introduced themselves to their new neighbors. They sampled their new, interesting food.

It was very different from what the cubs were used to.

But once they tried it, they thought it was delicious!

Most of the new families had cubs of their own. They were eager to make friends.

Soon, all of the cubs were playing, running, shouting, tumbling, and laughing happily together on the village green.

The cubs' parents got together, too. They talked and ate and drank and learned about each other.

It was fascinating to find out how folks lived all around the world!

By the end of the day, the Bear family felt as warm and loving about their new neighbors as they did about their old neighbors.

"I guess all bears are pretty much alike under the fur!" said Papa as they headed home.

The rest of the family, full of delicious food from around the world, certainly agreed!